Thomas Brewer

Memoir of Mr. Walter Scott

Thomas Brewer

Memoir of Mr. Walter Scott

Reprint of the original, first published in 1858.

1st Edition 2023 | ISBN: 978-3-37515-540-7

Salzwasser Verlag is an imprint of Outlook Verlagsgesellschaft mbH.

Verlag (Publisher): Outlook Verlag GmbH, Zeilweg 44, 60439 Frankfurt, Deutschland
Vertretungsberechtigt (Authorized to represent): E. Roepke, Zeilweg 44, 60439 Frankfurt, Deutschland
Druck (Print): Books on Demand GmbH, In de Tarpen 42, 22848 Norderstedt, Deutschland

MEMOIR

OF

MR. WALTER SCOTT,

Citizen and Plaisterer of London;

WITH

AN ACCOUNT OF THE

BLUE COAT CHARITY SCHOOL,

Founded and Endowed by him,

IN THE TOWN OF ROSS, HEREFORDSHIRE.

BY

THOMAS BREWER,

ONE OF THE COURT OF ASSISTANTS OF THE PLAISTERERS' COMPANY;

SECRETARY OF THE CITY OF LONDON SCHOOL.

LONDON:

PRINTED BY W. O. MITCHELL, 39, CHARING CROSS.

1858.

TO

THE MASTER,

WARDENS, AND COURT OF ASSISTANTS,

OF

THE WORSHIPFUL COMPANY OF PLAISTERERS,

𝕿𝖍𝖎𝖘 𝕸𝖊𝖒𝖔𝖗𝖎𝖆𝖑

OF THE LIFE AND BENEVOLENCE OF

A MEMBER OF THEIR BODY

IN A BYGONE AGE

IS RESPECTFULLY INSCRIBED,

BY

THEIR FAITHFUL FRIEND AND ASSOCIATE,

THOMAS BREWER.

5th January, 1858.

CONTENTS.

CONTENTS.

MEMOIR.

The genius and indefatigable labours of Scotland's great novelist and bard, have ensured for the name of WALTER SCOTT an imperishable celebrity and universal fame. Wherever that name is met with, it recalls to memory a man whose fertility of imagination and powers of description gained him the highest literary distinction—whose productions were so numerous and so varied as to make him one of the wonders of the age—who reared for himself, in his mansion of Abbotsford, a home so interesting and so peculiarly characteristic as to form a fit monument to his memory—and lastly, whose glorious career was unhappily clouded at its close by severe reverses and misfortunes.

These are some of the thoughts which are connected with the name of Walter Scott; but, uncommon though the name may be, the individual who is the object of them is neither the *only* one nor the *first* one who has borne it, or whose memory is worthy of being preserved. It has been borne by another person, who, though possessing no title to a place in the annals of literature, nor achieving for himself a wide popularity or an hereditary distinction, is yet deserving of honourable and grateful remembrance, as an exemplary benefactor to the public, and a promoter of sound and useful education amongst the poorer inhabitants of his native town.

The Walter Scott of whom it is proposed now to record some particulars was born in the year 1716, in the town of Ross, in Herefordshire, a few years before the close of the long life of that pattern of good works, John Kyrle, whose virtues were celebrated by the muse of Pope, and won for him the enduring title of "The Man of Ross."

He was the son of John Scott, whose occupation was that of a Carpenter and Joiner, and whose position in life was probably of rather a humble kind, since, in bringing up his son, he was glad to avail himself of the advantages to be procured from a small Charity School in the town, where a few children—boys and girls—were educated and clothed. This School was first established in 1717, the year following that in which Walter Scott was born, and was supported by public subscriptions. From some old account books which are still extant, it appears that, in the year 1726 (at which time Scott must. have been one of its scholars), the income of the School was so small as to amount only to £70. 15s., derived from subscriptions, and £4, interest of a legacy left by Mr. Kyrle, " the Man of Ross "; and the expenditure was as follows, viz. : —

		£.	s.	d.
For Clothing	. . .	30	1	11½
„ Apprenticing .	. .	8	2	1
„ Salary of Schoolmaster	.	18	0	0
„ Do. of Schoolmistress	.	10	0	0
„ Books and Paper .	.	4	12	11

Making a Total of . £70 16 11½

From this statement may be inferred the true character of the establishment, and also, that the number of children benefited by it, and the education they received, were both very limited. Small as must have been the scholastic advantages such an Institution could confer, it was the lot of Walter Scott to enjoy no others. We have his own testimony to this effect, given late in life (as will be seen hereafter); and yet the "little learning," as he himself terms it, which he there acquired, was not unproductive of good results, and he remembered it to the last with signal gratitude.

At the early age of thirteen, or thereabouts, Scott left his native town and came to London in search of employment: hoping, no doubt, to find in the busy metropolis some opportunity for the exercise of an honest industry by which he might acquire, as many a country lad had done before, a position of comfort and respectability, if not of absolute independence.

Fortunately for him he had an uncle living

in London, who at once took him into his employ, and taught him the business which he followed, as a Plaisterer.

Most persons have some knowledge of the nature of this business; but still it is, perhaps, not out of place to quote here what is said of it in a Publication which appeared in Scott's time, entitled "A General Description of all Trades, digested in alphabetical order; by which parents, guardians, and trustees, may with greater ease and certainty make choice of Trades agreeable to the capacity, education, inclination, strength, and fortune of the youth under their care." (London, 1747.) In this work, the description given of the business of a Plaisterer is as follows:—

"Plaisterers, the XLIVth [in precedency as a City Company].

"Theirs is one of the absolutely necessary Trades,

not only in completing new buildings, but in keeping them in repair, as well as making them clean; therefore is continually called on: and a clever, profitable business it is, take it throughout, though a dirty one; and not the most laborious.

"They take with an Apprentice five or ten pounds, who work from 6 to 6, in which hours a journeyman will earn from 2s. 6d. to 5s. Fifty pounds will furnish a Master with tools and stuff sufficient to begin to work with; and what he wants more, must be in proportion to the credit he thinks proper to give."

It does not appear whether Walter Scott was bound to his uncle as an apprentice, or not; although, having regard to the prevailing custom at that time, it would seem probable that he was. But if so, he did not acquire the Freedom of the City of London by such servitude; for, on the 28th of June, 1748, an Order was passed by the Court of Lord Mayor and Aldermen for his admission by Redemption;

by virtue whereof he was accordingly admitted on the 16th of September following, having on the preceding day been admitted by Redemption as a Freeman of the Company of Plaisterers, in accordance with the custom of the City, and the provisions of an Act of Common Council of the 19th of October, 1694, which required every person carrying on the business of a Plaisterer in London to become a Member of the Plaisterers' Company.

The connection with his uncle, once begun, seems to have continued uninterruptedly until severed by death, when, like many another faithful London apprentice or servant, he succeeded to his late master's business, and continued it on his own account until, after about thirty years' sedulous devotion to it, he was enabled to retire from it with an independent fortune, as the reward of his industry and good character.

His place of business was in Peterborough Court, Fleet Street, in the Parish of Saint Bride, and Ward of Farringdon Without.* It was of this Ward that the celebrated John Wilkes was Alderman; and when, after his exclusion from the House of Commons as representative for Middlesex, and his concurring with Aldermen Crosby and Oliver in committing a messenger of the House of Commons for arresting a citizen under a warrant from the Speaker, in violation of the privileges of the City, Wilkes and Alderman Townsend were put forward by the Livery at the Election for Lord Mayor in 1772, in opposition to Aldermen Halifax and Shakespeare, who were their seniors in office, but entertained different political

---

* He is named as assessed for these premises in a series of "Collectors' Books of the Impropriate Tithes and Augmentation Dues of St. Bride's Parish," in the City Library at Guildhall, the earliest of which is for 1748, and the latest for 1775.

sentiments, we find Mr. Walter Scott supporting by his vote the popular candidates, and helping to swell the majority which placed them on the poll immensely in advance of the two Aldermen whose views were more in accordance with the Government of the day.* From this circumstance, and from his being also, in a contested Election for Members of Parliament, one of the supporters of Mr. Alderman Sawbridge, a stanch friend of Wilkes, and who is described as " the unshaken advocate of Parliamentary Reform, and the sworn enemy to corruption," it may fairly be inferred that, in the political contests which were carried

---

* The Court of Aldermen, having to choose between Wilkes and Townsend, selected the latter, as senior of the two, to be Lord Mayor on this occasion. It appears that in this contest sixteen Liverymen of the Plaisterers' Company voted for Halifax and Shakespeare, and thirty-one for Wilkes and Townsend—the latter number including also that worthy benefactor to the Company, Mr. Wm. Roberts.

on so warmly in those days, Mr. Scott's predilections were generally in favour of the Opposition party.

Mr. Scott's admission as a Freeman of the Company of Plaisterers was followed by his attainment, at various intervals, of the higher grades in the Company — as Liveryman, Steward, Assistant, Upper Warden, and, eventually, Master, as will be seen by the following particulars gathered from the books of the Company, with the kind assistance of Mr. Henry Mott, the Clerk to the Company.

" 15*th September*, 1748.

"Walter Scott admitted to the Freedom of this Company by Redemption, in pursuance of the Lord Mayor's Order dated 28th June, 1748 . £0 19   6

"Fine for admission .   . 1   1   0"

" 9*th November*, 1752.

"Mr. Walter Scott was clothed [*i. e.*, with the

Livery], and paid by note, in twelve months from the 1st instant £8 0 0
And Clothing money in cash . . 0 5 0"

"13*th October*, 1756.

"Mr. Walter Scott, summoned to be Steward, agreed to pay the Fine, and prayed to be admitted into the Court of Assistants, and promised both Fines next Lord Mayor's Day."

"9*th November*, 1756.

"Mr. Walter Scott paid the Steward's Fine (£5), and, on his application, was admitted an Assistant; paying a Fine, to be excused Renter Warden, £18."

"12*th December*, 1765.

"Mr. Wise, the Master, having died, Mr. Jabez Read, Upper Warden, was elected instead; and Mr. Walter Scott was elected Upper Warden in place of Mr. Read."

"1*st July*, 1766.

"Mr. Walter Scott, Upper Warden, was elected Master."

When Mr. Scott found himself in a position to withdraw from the cares and anxieties of business, he went to live at Hendon, in Middlesex; but subsequently removed nearer to London, and took up his residence in Hornsey Lane, where he spent the remainder of his days. He had a wife, but no family. After passing the age of threescore years, being in circumstances of ease and comfort, and having his mind unoccupied by any duties or claims arising from kindred of his own, his thoughts turned towards the town of his birth, and he resolved to pay it a visit; and, from what occurred in consequence, this was probably done mainly under the influence of some benevolent intentions.

Just fifty years had elapsed from the time when he first left the place, and he had never seen it since. Whatever pleasure he may have derived from revisiting the scenes of his childhood, and recalling to memory the incidents of his early life, it is not likely that he enjoyed, after so long an interval, the gratification of meeting with many of the companions of his youth, or of those who knew him in his boyish days, and of exchanging with them an account of their respective careers. But if. *individuals* were wanting to share in his sympathies, there were certain *objects* in the place which could not fail to be of deep interest to him. The house in which his father dwelt—the School where he was educated—the venerable Church which he had been wont to attend—its Church-yard studded with memorials of those who had passed away during his long absence — the beautiful public walks which the "Man of Ross" had provided for the adornment of the town—and the River Wye, with the scenery of picturesque loveliness through which it flows —these, and many other things, would each in turn occupy his attention and his thoughts. Amongst the various impressions received during his visit, were some, in connection with the old School, which greatly pained him. By the gradual falling off of the subscriptions on which it depended for support, the School had become almost deserted and useless; in fact, it seems scarcely to have had more than a nominal existence. By way of stimulating those who had the management of it to renewed exertion for its support, he set them an example, by offering an annual contribution himself, in the terms of a memorandum, which he gave to the Treasurer, to the following · effect, viz.:—

" I promise to pay to the Charity School in Ross,
" as soon as it can be revived or brought to its
" former perfection, the sum of Five Guineas per
" annum, and to continue the same so long as the
" School continues.   Dated 13th March, 1779."

This offer seems to have been designed to ascertain whether the inhabitants could be moved to take a deeper interest than they had lately done in the affairs of the School, and by no means to have been the measure of the bounty which Mr. Scott contemplated bestowing himself; for it is recorded that, at this same visit, he declared in the presence of Mr. Newman (at that time a surgeon in Ross), and another gentleman, that *there should be a better Blue School in Ross than ever yet had been;* but he did not express the extent of his intentions.

Some years afterwards, however, he addressed the following letter to Mr. Keyse, of Ross, announcing his intention of providing more munificently for the Charity in which he felt so great an interest.

23

" Hornsey Lane, Highgate,

" 10th December, 1785.

" Sir,

" As I have no children, and as God has
" blest me with a small fortune, I have a mind to
" re-establish the Blue Coat Charity School, at Ross,
" as I had the little learning I have, there; and as
" I understand the School is very low, or quite come
" to nothing, I shall be glad if you will let me know
" in what manner the money must be secured to
" maintain it for ever.

" I am, &c.,

" Walter Scott.

" P.S.—I shall leave this by my Will, at my
" death."

Faithful to the promise thus given, Mr. Scott, in his Will, made within twelve months afterwards — after expressing a desire to be buried in the Parish Churchyard of Ross, upon his late father, or as near thereto as convenient —directed that his executors should pay, out of some part of his money in the Funds, the yearly sum of two hundred pounds towards the support of a School at Ross, at their discretion. This bequest is followed by one of one hundred pounds per annum to his wife, Sarah Scott, to be paid weekly during her life, if she should so long continue his widow. Amongst a number of legacies to his friends, amounting together to three thousand five hundred pounds, he left the following, viz.:—To three sisters named Cowmeadow, four hundred and fifty pounds each; fifty pounds to Ann Cowmeadow the elder; and three hundred pounds to Ann Harrod, who lived with him and his wife. He named, as his executors, Mr. Richard Crowther, of Boswell Court, surgeon; Mr. Roger Griffin; Mr. John Jordan, of Newington Butts; Mr. Thomas Grint, of Lincoln's Inn; Mr. James Yerworth; and

Mr. William Whitley; and left to them and several members of their families the following sums, viz.:—To Mr. Crowther, four hundred pounds. He forgave the debt due from Mr. Griffin, on condition that he should pay one hundred pounds to his (Mr. Griffin's) daughter within twelve months; and also left a legacy to Mrs. Griffin of one hundred pounds. To Mr. Jordan he left one hundred pounds; to Mr. Grint one hundred and fifty pounds, and one hundred pounds to his wife; to Mr. Yerworth one hundred pounds; and to Mr. Whitley fifty pounds. He also bequeathed his reversionary interest in two houses in Cursitor Street, which had been left him by his brother, in one case to James Scott, son of James Scott of Calne, in the county of Wilts, and in the other, to the sister of the said James Scott the younger. The residue of his property he bequeathed to his executors; and by a Codicil he desired them to provide mourning for six persons who are therein named.

Both the Will and the Codicil are dated the 2nd of December, 1786.

Mr. Scott died on the 4th of the same month; and the Will was proved, by all the Executors, in the Prerogative Court of the Archbishop of Canterbury, on the 7th. Conformably to his desire, his remains were removed to Ross for interment, where they arrived on the 19th of December; and over his grave, which is at the west end of the Churchyard, on the north side, is to be found a plain stone Monument, surmounted by an urn, and enclosed with iron rails, which bears the following simple inscription :—

I. H. S.

IN HOPE OF A BLESSED RESURRECTION,

HERE RESTETH FROM HIS LABOURS

WALTER SCOTT,

THE GRATEFUL

RESTORER OF THE BLUE COAT SCHOOL.

HE DEPARTED THIS LIFE ON THE

4TH DECEMBER, 1786,

AGED 70 YEARS.

From some cause or other, several years elapsed before the wishes and intentions of Mr. Scott, with regard to the School at Ross, were brought into full effect; they were eventually, however, thoroughly realized, in a manner no less to his honour than to the permanent benefit of the town.

It appears that, after his death, the Executors

set apart £6,666. 13*s*. 4*d*., New South Sea Annuities, to answer his charitable donation of two hundred pounds a year; and that in the year 1792 they purchased a piece of land, and shortly after began to erect on it a suitable School House. It is said in a Guide Book to the locality, published by Mr. Charles Heath, of Monmouth, in 1826, that on the day the School House was begun, "a public procession of the inhabitants was made through the town, preceded by a band of music, to honour the laying of the first stone; and for its prosperity all hearts seemed to join in one general joy."

Subsequently, a suit in Chancery was commenced for the purpose of establishing and regulating the Charity; and by a decree made on the 25th of January, 1793, it was ordered that the Charity should be established, and it was referred to the Master to approve of a scheme and to appoint proper Trustees.

In pursuance of this order, the Master, on the 22nd November, 1797, made his Report, certifying that he had approved of The Right Honourable Thomas Harley, Sir George Cornewall, Sir Hungerford Hoskins, and the Rev. Hugh Morgan, as Trustees; and he found that there was then standing in the name of the Accountant General the aforesaid sum of £6,666. 13s. 4d., New South Sea Annuities, and £900 cash in the Bank, besides a balance of £742. 4s. remaining in the hands of the Executors; that the then present funds of the Blue Coat School, in addition to the foregoing amounts, consisted of a rent-charge of £4. 10s. per annum issuing out of an estate at Sellack, and £200 Three per Cent. Bank Annuities which had been purchased with money arising from the said annuity and from benefactions, &c.; and that he had approved of a scheme as therein set forth.

This Report being confirmed, the Cause came on to be heard before the Lord Chancellor on the 2nd of May, 1798, for further directions: when it was ordered (amongst other things) that a sum which, with the balance previously stated to be in the hands of the Executors, would make up one thousand pounds, should be paid to them in respect of the expense of purchasing the ground and building the School House; and that the ground and buildings, together with all moneys, should be transferred to the Trustees, and a proper deed be prepared for carrying the scheme into effect.

Such a deed was accordingly executed on the 23rd August, 1798. The first Meeting of the Trustees and Governors was held on the 19th November following; thirty boys and thirty girls were then elected, and a Committee appointed to superintend the preparation of the clothing, and the School was opened on the 5th of January, 1799.

The scheme which was approved by the Court of Chancery contains the fullest directions for the management of the Charity in every respect.

It declares that the School shall for ever be called "Walter Scott's Charity School." It provides for a constant succession of Trustees, in whom shall be vested the property of the Charity; and for associating with them, for the purposes of general management, a number of Governors, including the Bishop of the Diocese, the two representatives for the county, the two Churchwardens and Overseers of the Parish of Ross, and all benefactors to the School. There is to be one Schoolmaster and one Schoolmistress, who are to be chosen by the Trustees and Governors, and are to reside in the apartments provided for them in the School House. There are to be so many boys and girls in the School as the income will extend to clothe and educate, who are to be instructed in reading, writing, and arithmetic — the girls in plain needlework—and all of them in the grounds and principles of the Christian religion. No child is to be admitted under the age of six years, nor continue after the age of fourteen. The scholars must be natives of the parish of Ross, and either orphans, or the children of settled inhabitants of the parish of Ross in indigent circumstances; unless there should not be a sufficient number of that description who should apply to partake of the Charity, in which case children not born in the parish, but whose parents should be settled there, and in distressed circumstances, may be chosen. Children related to Walter Scott, who shall be equal objects of the Charity with others seeking the benefit thereof, shall have the preference.

The Clergyman ordinarily doing duty at the Parish Church of Ross is to be allowed annually one guinea for preaching a sermon on the 4th of December, being the anniversary of the death of Walter Scott, in commemoration of his bounty; and a dinner is to be provided annually on the same day for the scholars, at the expense of the Charity.

The children are to attend the Parish Church of Ross, with the Master and Mistress, every Sunday morning and afternoon, and on certain other days in the year; and upon every day on which they do not attend Divine Service, the eldest of the scholars is to read a form of prayer, to be approved by the Rector, and to be repeated by all the other scholars, offering up their most fervent thanks to Almighty God for the blessings he has bestowed upon them through their Benefactor, and after that a Psalm of thanksgiving.

It is also directed what shall be the hours of attendance, what books and articles of clothing shall be supplied to each scholar (a distinction being made in the dress of the boys in the last year, previous to their leaving the School), and that all the scholars shall wear a white medal, or badge, with an inscription in black letters, " Walter Scott's Charity."

The number of scholars has generally been thirty boys and thirty girls. The School Building is described by the Commissioners of Charities as convenient and extensive, including a comfortable house for the Master and Mistress; and it appears, by their Report, that the Charity is administered in close conformity to the scheme established by the Court of Chancery.

The particulars which have been gathered

and put together in the foregoing pages, of the personal history of the individual to whose bounty the public is indebted for this excellent Charity, are too scanty and too unimportant to possess much interest apart from this crowning act of his life. They furnish, however, a striking example of what industry and good principles will enable a man to achieve, for the advantage both of himself and his fellow-creatures; and it is hoped they may not be altogether unworthy of preservation in connection with the rise and progress of an Institution of so useful a character — one which sheds enduring honour upon the memory of its Founder, and justifies us in placing upon the long roll of benefactors to mankind the name of

WALTER SCOTT,

CITIZEN AND PLAISTERER OF LONDON.

NOTE.

The sources from which the foregoing particulars have been gathered are as follow :—

Heath's Excursion down the Wye from Ross to Monmouth.

Reports of Charity Commissioners, No. XXXII., Part 2, Page 76.

A General Description of all Trades, &c. 1747. Page 168.

Proceedings of Court of Aldermen, Ladbroke Mayor.

Tithe Collectors' Books for the Parish of St. Bride, 1748—1775.

List of Liverymen who polled in the Election for Lord Mayor, 1772.

List of Liverymen who voted for Mr. Alderman Sawbridge at the Election of Members of Parliament, 1784.

City Biography, Second Edition. 1800.

Minute Books, &c. of the Company of Plaisterers.

Will of Mr. Walter Scott, in Prerogative Office, Doctors' Commons.

Gentleman's Magazine for 1787. Vol. 57, Part I., Page 90.